Go Hiking

CARY WOOD AND
CECILIA TURNER

Morgan James
The Entrepreneurial Publisher™

NEW YORK

Davis And Pop Go Hiking

Published in New York, New York, by Morgan James Publishing. Morgan James and The Entrepreneurial Publisher are trademarks of Morgan James, LLC. www.MorganJamesPublishing.com

The Morgan James Speakers Group can bring authors to your live event. For more information or to book an event visit The Morgan James Speakers Group at www.TheMorganJames-SpeakersGroup.com.

A **free** eBook edition is available
with the purchase of this print book.

CLEARLY PRINT YOUR NAME ABOVE IN UPPER CASE

Instructions to claim your free eBook edition:
1. Download the BitLit app for Android or iOS
2. Write your name in **UPPER CASE** on the line
3. Use the BitLit app to submit a photo
4. Download your eBook to any device

ISBN 978-1-63047-068-5 paperback
ISBN 978-1-63047-069-2 eBook

Cover Design by:
Chris Treccani
www.3dogdesign.net

Interior Design by:
Bonnie Bushman
bonnie@caboodlegraphics.com

In an effort to support local communities and raise awareness and funds, Morgan James Publishing donates a percentage of all book sales for the life of each book to Habitat for Humanity Peninsula and Greater Williamsburg.

Get involved today, visit
www.MorganJamesBuilds.com

Habitat
for Humanity®
Peninsula and
Greater Williamsburg
Building Partner

**"M**om", Davis called out.

"Are you okay Davis," Mom asks?

"Yes Mom but I'm just too excited to sleep. What time is Pop picking me up in the morning? I don't want to sleep late and miss him."

Pop is Davis' grandfather and he was coming early in the morning to take Davis hiking. Davis had never been hiking before and really didn't understand what it was all about but he was still excited. He knew it had something to do with being outdoors and possibly seeing animals along the way.

"Pop is coming at 6:00 in the morning which is very early so you need to get some sleep. You are going to have a great time with Pop if you get a good night's sleep. You will need lots of energy to do all of that hiking," Mom tells him.

"Okay Mom. I love you. Goodnight."

The next morning Mom came in Davis' room and said, "Wake up Davis. Pop is here and it's time to go hiking." Davis jumped out of bed and ran to see Pop. Pop gave him a big hug and said, "Good morning, Davis. Are you ready to go hiking with me?" Davis looked at Pop and said, "I sure am. Are we leaving now?"

Pop said, "Right after breakfast. It's important we eat a good breakfast because we are going to get a lot of exercise today." Mom had prepared a wonderful breakfast for them and Davis cleaned his plate. He wanted to make sure he did everything Pop told him to do.

After breakfast Davis ran to the bathroom to brush his teeth. Then he started changing his clothes. His mom had bought him a new outfit to hike in. He had green hiking shorts with pockets and a tee shirt to wear that would be cool because it was a hot summer day. The neatest things though, were a vest that had lots of pockets to put things in and waterproof hiking boots. With the boots on he could walk through shallow water and mud and not get his feet wet. He hurried up and got dressed and then he told Pop he was ready to go.

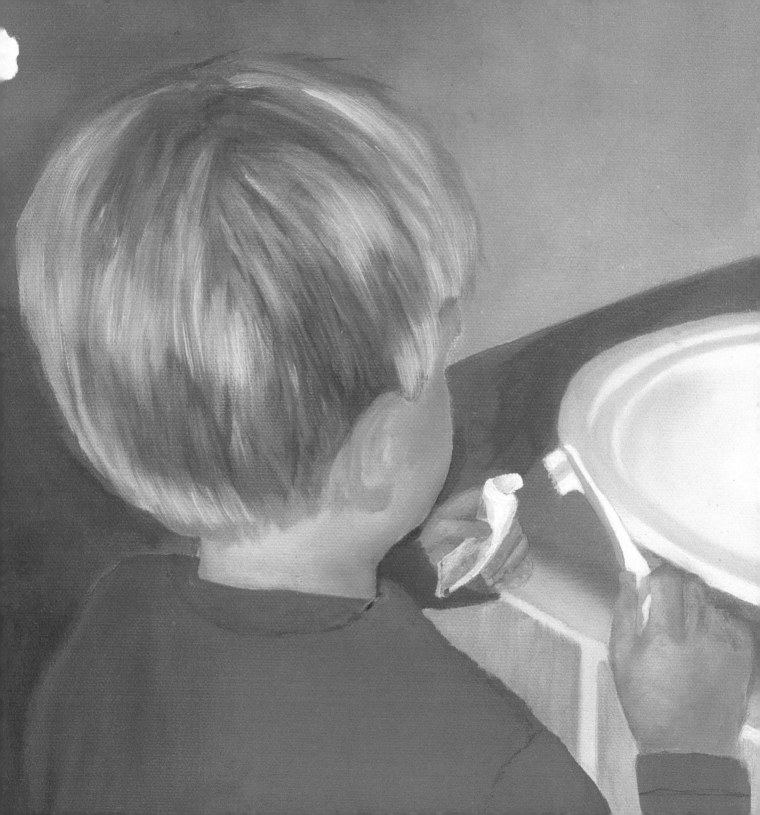

Davis kissed his Mom and Dad goodbye and he and Pop climbed into the truck. They put their seatbelt on and took off for their first hike together.

Pop tells Davis that they will be walking the whole time and it will be a very long walk. If Davis gets tired he needs to tell Pop so that they can sit down somewhere and rest. He tells Davis that he has a backpack for Davis to carry and Pop has one too. Davis' backpack had snacks for them to eat along the way and peanut butter and jelly sandwiches for lunch. Yum!

Pop's backpack had bug spray and a camera to take lots of pictures with, a compass for directions and binoculars to see things far off. He had some matches in case they needed to build a fire and plenty of water in a thermos bottle for both of them because it's good for your body to drink a lot of water when you are outside. Pop wanted Davis to know that it was very important that they come prepared with things that will help them.

Pop also told Davis that he needed to stay right with Pop the whole time. There might be some dangerous areas or wild animals and Pop wanted Davis to be safe.

They parked the truck and got out. Pop reached in the back and pulled out their backpacks. He handed Davis one that was just the right size for Davis to carry. It was blue, Davis' favorite color. Pop helped him put it on his back and tightened the straps so it would fit right. Then Pop put his backpack on. It was much heavier than the one Davis was carrying but Pop could handle it. Pop had some sunscreen that he put on Davis and himself to keep the hot sun from hurting their skin and he also took out some bug spray and put some on their legs and arms to keep away the mosquitoes. They were all set to go.

Pop locked the truck and said, "Are you ready, Davis?" Davis looked at Pop and said a big, "YES SIR"! He couldn't wait to get started. Pop said, "First let's say a prayer to God." Pop bowed his head and Davis did too. Pop prayed, "Dear God. Please keep Davis and me safe while we go hiking. Let us enjoy Your beautiful earth that You created. Amen." Davis said, "Amen" too and off they went.

At first they had to climb a very steep hill. The path was very narrow but it was easy to follow. They stopped along the way and rested for a minute. Davis was breathing hard but he wanted to keep going. They climbed some more and came to a place where they could stand on some granite and look out. You could see for a long way. There was a road with cars on it and Davis thought the cars looked like his toy cars at home. Pop pulled out some raisins and water and they ate a little snack. When they finished they made sure they put all of their trash in Davis' backpack so they wouldn't litter. It's always important to not throw your trash on the ground because animals may come by and try to eat it and it would make them very sick.

op said, "It's time to move on." They climbed up the path some more. They saw squirrels and chipmunks all along the way. Davis heard a noise and asked Pop "What is that." Pop said it was water coming down a waterfall making a rushing sound. They were going to hike to the waterfall so Davis could see it. He had never seen a waterfall before. Davis noticed the air around them getting cooler and cooler and the noise getting louder and louder. All of a sudden they stepped into a clearing and there it was. It was the biggest thing Davis had ever seen. The water would spill over the top and crash to the bottom. When it crashed it would spray a mist of water over him and Pop. It felt so good. Pop found a big rock for them to sit on where they could watch it. Davis looked around and saw a squirrel sitting on a stump eating some nuts and a little chipmunk close by.

Pop told Davis to take his backpack off and it was time to eat their lunch. Davis looked inside and there were the peanut butter and jelly sandwiches. Pop asked God to bless their food and thanked Him for letting them see the beautiful waterfall. Then they ate their sandwiches. That was the best peanut butter and jelly sandwich Davis had ever eaten. Even though he had a big breakfast he was hungry after all that walking and climbing.

After they ate Pop let Davis do some exploring. He went down to the edge of the water that wasn't dangerous and found some small stones. The water had made them smooth and shiny. They felt good in his hands. He played a long time in the water and with the rocks. He would throw the rocks into the water and they would make a big "kerplunk" sound. That was fun. He found a special rock that he thought was extra shiny so he put it in one of the pockets in his vest to take home. He knew just where he wanted to put it so he would always remember this day.

He and Pop walked up stream a little bit to look around and they saw a raccoon drinking water from the edge. He looked like he had a black mask around his eyes. Pop got out his camera and took a picture.

Pop said, "It's time to go. It's a long walk back to the truck." Davis hated to leave but he didn't argue. They started back down the path. Going down was much easier than going up! Pop whispered, "Davis stop. Look through the bushes to the right." Davis stopped and looked and there were three deer. It was a mama deer called a doe and two baby deer called fawns. They were eating and didn't see Davis and Pop. They had fluffy white tails that stuck up in the air. Davis liked watching them eat. All of a sudden the mama deer saw Davis and Pop and she quickly ran in the other direction. The baby deer followed her. Davis thought that was funny and laughed as he watched their white tails disappear in the wood.

They kept going down the path and that was fun. Davis could go much faster downhill instead of uphill. Pop saw a big rock and told Davis it was time for a snack. They sat on the rock and each of them ate a big juicy red apple. It tasted so good. Davis looked at Pop and said, "Pop this has been the best day I've ever had. Can we go hiking again soon." Pop told Davis, "It's been a great day for me too. I promise we will do a lot of hiking in the future. I'll show you some of my favorite places."

They made it back to the truck and put their backpacks in the back. Davis put his seat belt on and Pop pulled out of the parking place. It didn't take long before Davis was fast asleep. He was very tired but he was very happy. He dreamed of taking more hikes with Pop soon and seeing more things he'd never seen before. Hiking was fun and the best part was spending the day outdoors with his Pop.

THE END

Printed in the USA
CPSIA information can be obtained
at www.ICGtesting.com
JSHW041935140824
68134JS00012B/124